Roots Before Wings

DARRAGHA FOSTER

ACKNOWLEDGMENTS

Thanks go to JSS for sharing her story.

prologue

Jada watched Granny Treemaven roll the bones across a scarlet cloth. Well used and threadbare, the cloth had been witness to countless acts of fortune telling because Granny was over a hundred years old. Her thin fingers spoke of a long life filled with hard work and her eyes—her cloudy eyes acted as mirrors. "So you is a witch, child? You hear their voices and can smell the old ones on the wind?"

Jada nodded. "Yes'm." She was wiser than she should have been for her fourteen years. It happened in the hills. A hard-scrabbled life compounded by booze, blood, and abuse made a girl a woman too fast.

"I see hurt upon you baby girl. Hurt that you hide. Hurt that eats at you like a dragon eats the roots of the World Tree, slowly, but thoroughly."

Jada flinched. "World Tree?" *I haven't mentioned that vision to a soul. Not one.*

"Your blood is Scandinavian, yes? German, too, I figure."

Jada nodded. "Guess that's where this mop of blonde hair and blue eyes come from. Isn't from the Cherokee blood, I reckon."

"You seek answers to questions and lessons of magic that can only come to you by your ancestors and their gods. Do you know the gods of your fathers and mothers?"

"My mama went to St. Sophia's Catholic church, ma'am. My daddy worships the bottle."

"No. Your foremothers and forefathers. In the days of old. Days gone by that are even older than me."

"Mama used to read those stories to me. The legends. She called it *the lore*. But she always said like the little *l* like it shoulda been a capital one. Like with the big B in the word Bible. Lore, with a capital L."

"Never knew your mama well, child. But she was a smart woman. The Lore of those bedtime stories are the Bible to your late kinfolk over there in Norway and Denmark. And who's to say those old gods aren't as real as the Wampus Cat we all see skulking 'round here on the dark of the moon or those miracles of Jesus at the tent revivals? They walk the earth today. Answer your questions and guide you, they can. If you know how to call them."

"Are those the voices I hear?"

"Mayhaps."

"They have whispered of the World Tree to me. And the dragon. Nidhogg. They call it Nidhogg."

"I know of that beast. What else do you hear?"

Jada sighed. "Roots before wings. That before I can fly I need to grow roots. Then they show me the dragon gnawing on the roots of my world tree. I need to make peace with the dragon. But defeating it won't stop it. Only embracing it will."

"Show you things, too, do they? And don't fib. The bones tell me the truth. This old hollar witch just needs to hear it from your own lips."

"Flame Hair. I see a man—his hair is made of fire."

Granny nodded. "Scarred lips like someone sewed his lying mouth shut?" Jada nodded.

"I know him. His name is Loki. He's a rascal, that one. He's a god of change. Big change. Change such as you need to be strong, girl. Change strong enough to defeat the demons plaguing you. Make offerings of blood and sweets. Old Flame Hair can't resist sweets. But mind you, his kiss is as sweet as honey and as intoxicating as hard liquor. He traps folks in a net and keeps them there until they embrace change."

"Loki? Loki from the lore?"

Granny raised a bony finger to her lips. "Don't invoke his name here, girl. I'm too old to deal with the likes of him. I fell under his spell decades ago. I can feel him on the breeze even now. Go into the woods. Make your offerings. I won't be able to speak with you about these things again. This is my last night."

"Can you tell me about him?"

"No. I can't. He's the god of change, child. He is different for every woman. Look, I want you to return to my home tomorrow. You come back here and take whatever you want from my stores. Take my cloth and bones. Take my books and spell bottles. And girl..."

"Yes?"

"You need to keep your blood for yourself and the gods. That drunken father of yours is evil to the core and I want you to leave home just as soon as you can. He is full of bad magic. You get yourself out."

"I don't have anywhere to go."

"Old Flame Hair will see to that. Your work with him is just beginning. But remember—it's all about air and wings with him. Roots will come later. And that's when the sickness in your heart will heal up proper."

"Should I call anyone tomorrow, Granny? When I return and find you..."

"I don't fear death dear. Go on and say the words. 'When you find me dead.' Yes. Call the undertaker' son. He knows what

I want. Paid his daddy fifty years ago to take care of me upon passing. My instructions are on file."

"Yes, ma'am."

"After you take what you want from here, and my body has been buried, torch this place. I want you to conjure spirits of blue flame and dance in the glow. Mayhaps you and that young man, Jimmy O'Hara." Jada felt her face flush.

"He's a good young man. Marry him if you can. His mama was a spirit worker and he understands women such as you. I know you and that Jimmy have shared a few kisses and said some promises to one and other. That's kin to taking an oath, girl. I tell you, marry him or go without a husband, for few men will understand your carrying on with the likes of old Flame Hair. That Jimmy O'Hara will love you in spite of your being a spirit working hollar witch."

Jada nodded. "Yes'm. That's a tall order to fill, and I'm underage to wed Jimmy proper."

"No matter. Just cross the state line and you and he can wed. Not like your daddy will stop you. Now, git that skinny ass of yours to the big trees in the heart of the hollar and make me proud magic. Tell old Flame Hair something for me?"

"All right."

Granny smiled a toothless, lascivious smile. "Tell him thank you." Jada turned to leave.

Granny called out after her. "Keep your true name to yourself when working with the old ones."

"Why?"

"Jest do it. Trust old Granny now."

"Yes'm."

Granny was if nothing else, cryptic. It sometimes left her a bit unnerved, talking things through with the old woman—but there was none better in the region to put her feet on the correct path. God knows daddy didn't have a clue and mama was long gone. Jada corrected herself. Gods know. *Gods.* The trek into the heart of the hollar wasn't difficult. In fact, trekking that deep into the forest brought a sense of calm that she rarely felt. Mama's ashes were scattered in the woods and daddy was too drunk far too much of the time to follow her into the thickness. The voices whispered at her as she made her way to the tree. The big tree—nine tree trunks grown together into one. Some folks called it a cathedral tree for its resemblance to a bank of church organ pipes.

Only little streams of light pierced the dark coolness and thick canopy. She thought it looked like a straw caddy at the sporting goods store soda counter. *God has a handful of straws in heaven and is pushing them through the trees to suck up the forest floor.* She dug her heels in before the cathedral tree, and shivered in the half-light.

"All right y'all, this is kind of impromptu. I'll figure out how to do things proper later on. Right now, I ask that you listen to me and help me fly away from this place so that I can learn the things I need to learn." She pricked her finger with a safety pin and squeezed out a few drops of blood on to an exposed root. She took a restaurant peppermint out of her jacket pocket and crushed it under foot. "Hail gods of my ancestors."

The air pressure changed. She felt it prickle her flesh like someone had dropped ice down her shirt. She fell to the ground as vertigo hit and vomited as the forest floor wobbled beneath her.

Out of the corner of her eye she caught the shadowed form of a man. He moved like a dancer; tall, lithe, almost magical. Make that very magical. His head was crowned with flame.

"Offering accepted, princess. Our lessons begin." He lifted her to her feet. "And when you are of age, we shall wed."

Jada gazed into his hazel eyes. "I want to marry Jimmy. Granny said that it should be so."

"And so you shall. You shall be his earthly wife. And mine in realms not of this earth."

"Am I dead?"

"Ah, no. You are quite alive. Your body sleeps now beneath the cathedral tree. Your spirit is with me. We shall skip between the raindrops and waltz across the vault of heaven."

"Are you a god?"

"I am. I am your god. My name is Loki."

ten years later

Jada collapsed into the over-stuffed sofa next to her husband of ten years. She let her head fall onto his shoulder.

"What's wrong, honey?" Jim asked. "You don't snuggle unless you are stressing out about something."

"I do too snuggle," Jada replied.

"No. You're too busy with the kids and the house to catch a breath. I'm lucky I get a few minutes to hold you after sex before you talk about the construction on our new place or some other life event that can't be put on the back burner for an hour of afterglow. So, what is it, dear? Animal? Vegetable? Spiritual?"

"Spiritual."

"Your invisible boyfriend being a pain in the ass again?" Jim asked.

"I wish you wouldn't call him that, but yes."

"I'm a man, and a jealous one at that. It took me a while to accept that I have to share you with a spirit—"

Jada interrupted, "A god. Loki."

Jim slid his well-muscled left arm around his wife. "A god, yes. Thank goodness Loki's not a bloodthirsty Titan of old or anything like that." He muted the TV.

"He's worse sometimes, honey. And I think you've been watching too much of that History Channel special on Greece. We're Northern Tradition pagans, not Hellenics."

Jimmy comforted his wife. "Look, sweetie, I believe in you and trust you to wake up beside me every morning, no matter where he takes you in your dreams. I fell in love with a god-bothered pagan. It goes with the territory. I knew about

Loki when we crossed the state line to get married. I have never denied your work with the gods and I never will."

"I love you, Jimmy. It's hard for me to show and even harder to say—but I do. I'm lucky I stopped long enough to say 'yes' to you all those years ago. And you knew about my issues and still proposed. Part of the work I do with the gods is to conquer my self-imposed limitations, especially when it comes to love. Pretty sure that will benefit our marital community. We've made a good life. Even with having babies, I finished my degree and you moved up to foreman of the biggest construction company in the region. I thank Loki for my life." She rubbed a scar across her forearm. "Before Loki and before you—I had nothing but pain filling my days."

Jimmy took her hand. "I love you, too, baby. I ain't going nowhere. I knew when I proposed and you accepted that it wasn't going to be an easy ride. Hell, we were married three months before you told me 'I love you.' I married a mountain hollar witch with a streak of melancholy and I accept that. I'm sure you put some spell on me to get me to propose, anyways."

Jada smiled. "Only a little one."

"Loki was just a part of the package it took me a little longer to accept. Just tell old Flame Hair that he needs to do right by you or I'm going to find him and kick his ass."

"Sometimes the right thing hurts. That's where I am now. He's pushed me into a corner. A fight or flight situation."

"About time. You've been working with him for what...ten years? Longer? Divine therapy—bah. At least he can get you to discuss your crappy past. I gave up asking you about your childhood—not because I don't care—but because I was tired of you coming unglued whenever I brought up the subject. It may just be time for you to put up your dukes and throw a few punches on that astral plain of yours. And as much as it bugs me, I know that—especially with those horny Norse gods—that your battle plan might come at the end of Loki's dick."

"Sex isn't about sex with them. It looks and feels like it, but it's really about the exchange of sacred energy. I sometimes wonder if the same exchange could be had by his putting a finger into my ear—though that has certainly not been his preference." She sighed. "Truthfully, Jimmy...I want to hold up a white flag and go into hibernation. It's far less challenging to surrender."

"Sex isn't about sex with *them*?" Jimmy asked. "There's been more than Loki?"

"I can't control who wants to exchange energy with me in my dreams. Every now and then I get swooped by one of them. Sometimes the lesson is clear. Sometimes it's not. Today, in fact, I've felt another presence trying to touch me. It's a very earthy energy. It leaves a flavor in my mouth that reminds me of eating baby carrots right out of the soil in the garden."

"That doesn't sound too attractive to me. Daddy don't like dirty veggies. But if it turns out it's one of those hot Valkyrie chicks wantin' to bone you, invite me to watch."

"I'll see what I can do, honey." Jada sat upright. "You know...the kids are awfully quiet."

"They must be plotting something. Want me to go check on them?"

"Please. I'll go start dinner."

"Maybe I'll take the kids out to the pond later—give you some time to straighten things out, meditatively speaking."

"That would be nice. Thank you."

"Don't forget to give Loki my message. My foot. His ass."

"He knows, honey. I'm sure he heard you."

* * * *

In those realms found only between drops of rain or riding on the trails of laughter, Loki attempted a hard swig from his tankard. *Contents gone, nothing left. Drained dry. Damn.* He set it on the floor and hung his head over his knees. Any reasonable upright posture was contrary to his state of drunkenness. If he balanced himself correctly, he wouldn't list too far and end up on the floor, though he knew that was probably next. *I am drunk. I am very, very drunk. I will drink until I reach oblivion for it is there that I am unburdened by love.* He sighed and wished his cup full. It remained empty.

Of course, if I'm already on the floor I could crawl to the bar to refill my cup. Damned early morning self-service. Blasted early hour. Damned serving wenches are off duty. He corrected himself. Firstly, it was no longer considered apropos to refer to them as wenches, and secondly, men also served the gods, a twenty-first century development. Women had always fought in rank and phalanx, but men had never before carried tankards of ale for the gods. Times change. People change. Even the gods change. *I am the god of change and I cannot yet face the ones vexing my world.* He chuckled, to himself he hoped. Of course, there was no expectation of privacy in the common halls of Asgard.

His thoughts were interrupted by a pair of large motorcycle boots which stepped into his pity pot. He angled his aching head upward to see stout legs in denim and leather chaps. The waistline bore a familiar symbol, a lightning bolt belt buckle and holstered like a six shooter, the *Mjolnir*. Thor's hammer. "What's so funny over here in the corner, Loki?"

"Be a doll and get me another beer, will you, Thor?"

He picked up Loki's empty cup. "Join me at a table. I feel you are troubled and my nephew says I am to render aid. Forseti says there is justice to be had and that I am to play a part in its dispensing."

"Will your aid involve alcohol? And Forseti is a somber man always seeing the worst in things. His portents of the future bore me, which is one reason I chose to drink in this corner than at the bar with my brethren."

"I'll fill your tankard, and listen to you complain about those who mean you well if you wish. Besides, Forseti has left for home. Can you walk?"

"I had decided that perhaps any form of forward motion might cause me to vomit or fall embarrassingly to my knees. So, I think not."

Thor slapped Loki on the shoulder. "I'm certain that you have been on your knees in this hall before. Crawl if need be, but get yourself to a table." The thunder god turned and laughed.

Loki looked up. He winced as his bloodshot eyes reacted to the first light of day streaming into the hall. "Dawn. As unwelcome a sight as any I have seen of late." He stood and took a moment to steady himself. "I can do this."

No. He could not. Loki fell to the floor with a great thud. He lay still for a moment. No-one rushed to his aid. He did hear Thor laugh in the background. Fortunately, he had landed near a bench, said bench being beside a table. He pulled himself up. He grasped the table with both hands and envisioned his butt taking root. He sat upright, head swaying from the beer and the fall. "Where's my drink, Thor?"

"Yes, Loki. I bring it now. But it is half-ale, for if you drink any more fullstrength, I'm afraid you might make a pass at me."

Loki took the offered pint. "Wouldn't be the first time." He took a swig. "We've had sex, haven't we Thor?I remember you were wearing a dress and I—"

"That is not a topic for open discussion, Loki. Now, is it a wife or a plot that vexes thee?"

The fire god lifted his glass and made a mock salute. "It is a woman. A wife. Or rather a woman I had assumed by now would be my wife by blood oath and not just promise."

"And the name of your resistant bride, sir?" Thor held his tankard aloft, waiting for Loki's reply.

"Jada."

"I salute Jada, wife of Loki, for causing him such strong consternation that he kisses the floor of this hall rather than her lips this fine morning."

"Oh, I kissed her lips, all right. Those above and below. I felt," Loki leaned in, and whispered, "She displayed trepidation at my touch."

Thor laughed. "Really? Is she mortal or Jotun or some species in between?"

"Mortal. As lovely a human woman as I have beheld. She rivals the morning sun, and burns just as hot."

"Ah, she has a temper."

"To match only your own, Thor."

"How long have you been betrothed?"

Loki pulled his goatee thoughtfully. "While she married her mortal spouse, she took secret vows to me in her heart. Ten years ago. We began our work together only weeks before she wed."

"No an oath-taking then? No formal vows?" Thor asked.

"Only those of a woman in love and whose love was returned in kind."

"And now?"

"We've reached an impasse. She finds my lessons difficult to bear. We are at the verge of a breakthrough and she backs away. Fear is a powerful master. She has no reason to distrust or fear me, yet the fear in which she has encased herself causes her to shun challenges while blaming me for the obstacles. I always offer the solution in the hand opposite the problem. I showed her that hand, Thor—and she ran. Her past must be remembered and embraced before she can step into the light of divine relationships, much less make her mortal ones more enjoyable."

Thor nodded. "Interesting."

"She is a smoldering forest fire. There is so much untapped passion in her. I have tried to bring it forth, to allow it freedom. But she reins it in and hides her light as she feels some of her passions are so strong, they could be her undoing if not controlled."

"By you?"

Loki nodded. "Yes."

"Perhaps she needs a slower hand or a guide who speaks plainly."

Loki pushed his cup away. "Is there any coffee? The morning commissary shift has arrived. Can you get us some, Thor?"

Thor turned in his seat and motioned for assistance. "May we have two coffees, please? Cream and sugar."

Loki didn't look up. "Extra sugar."

Thor continued. "Extra sugar."

The worker waved at Thor and poured two large mug of steaming, black coffee. He set them on a tray with a small pitcher and a great mound of sugar cubes.

"They know how we take our coffee, Loki. The commissary staff cook and clean for us."

"I'm married to the head housekeeper. She is magnificent."

"Perhaps you should devote more attention to her and leave Jada to her mortal spouse."

"I don't know what to do about Jada, this is true. Her mortal is a good man, but he doesn't challenge her. And as for Kathryn...the housekeeping overseer, I am her second husband. She is first oathed to Freyr."

"An unusual balance of power."

"Indeed," Loki said. He reached for his coffee before the tray was placed on the table. "He is growth and renewal and I am the shadow of same...challenge and life-changing destruction. Our wife is often quite tired from working with us."

"I've seen Freyr's hand tool. Any woman would be fatigued after a bout with that monster."

"Yes, well. I'll make no comments there. Perhaps I should introduce Jada to Freyr."

Thor shook his head. "I don't think a fertility god would be any less of a pain in the ass for her than you are."

Loki dropped six sugar cubes into his mug, one after the other. He watched the ripples' wake and caught site of Thor's reflection. "How many wives do you currently have, Thor?"

"Sif, of course. And I am honored to be the divine spouse of several mortal women. I've a few husbands, too, but not as many as you and Odin."

"Jada needs someone like you, Thor. You are steady and pragmatic. You are not prone to embellishment. Even your renowned temper has dimmed over the centuries."

"Fewer giants to smash."

"Jada and I are not oathed, thereby, for me to take a step away and for you to enter her life is not oath-breaking, nor is it against the code of *frith and fulltrui*. I can introduce you..."

Thor blew across the top of his mug. "Why should I want that which you cannot handle?"

"No, look. It's perfect. She is more suited to you than I. I love her, to be sure, but she no longer responds to my voice or my touch. The lessons are going unlearned for want of another teacher. Thor, I think it is you. She needs you." Loki perked up. "Perhaps just an association with you will allow her to ground. If you marry her—she will be unstoppable. Oh, indeed. What a brilliant idea!"

Thor slid his motorcycle goggles farther back on his head. "Really?"

"Yes."

"Tell me more. I'm not opposed to the idea. I often provide mortal women with the strong sense of stability they need in a god."

"Yes, your stable hand in lessons of heart and spirit."

"Let me watch her from the shadows and I will determine if I am a good fit. Will you go to her today?" Thor asked.

"When she meditates, I will answer her call."

"Does she recognize us outside of meditation or sleep?"

Loki nodded. "Yes."

Thor leaned in. "Is she comely? Bonny and buxom in the bed with a brain as well-rounded as her body?"

Loki nodded. "She earned a masters degree while pregnant with her second child. She's smarter and cleverer than most. And for a woman who has suffered at the unkind hands of too many mortal men, she does not hide her passions too deeply. Sometimes it's taken me more than the usual amount of effort to draw from her lips the cry of sweet satisfaction I so love to hear in my wives, but she isn't frigid, if that's what you mean. Another few weeks and I'd have her embracing her past and conquering it. Fear has destroyed us, Thor."

"Well, I'm always ready to help a brother god. Send me a signal when you go to her. I'll listen for it." Thor paused, musing over his mug. "Jada...that isn't her real name, is it?"

"No. That's what she asked me to call her. She protects her true name as if it were part of a dragon's treasure mound, all hidden and safe. I believe she fears recognizing her true self. Given no name, she feels no pain. But then there is no growth—nor joy or love or rage or—"

Thor interrupted. "Did you smite her abuser?"

Loki took a deep breath. "I feel inclined to embellish my smiting of them a bit after all the drink. But yes. I put the fear of god into him, so to speak. Hail, my beloved daughter, Hel, Queen of the Underworld. She has done me a great service by inflicting the worst kind of punishment upon him."

"He torments her after death?"

"His hold on her is painful to witness. It's her own father, Thor. He was a vile man of unholy appetites. And he haunts her every breath. Hel has a very special dark place in the underworld for the likes of him. Perhaps you will make her feel secure enough to divulge further detail that will give voice and name to the crimes committed upon her. To face them is to conquer them. But today, she runs away rather than face the truth."

"Truly, only Jada can combat the shadow of her abusers. Naming them is but the first step to victory. It could be that Sif's gentle hand can guide her, too. Hail Sif, my wife whom I love above all others. That's not to say, of course, that any of my other spouses suffer due to want." "Sif is a special creature, indeed." Thor grumbled.

"Oh, do not get your dander up, Thor. Any dalliance between Sif and I happened long before the second dawn of our kind. We haven't so much as glanced at each other in centuries."

"You no longer find her attractive?" Thor asked.

Loki mulled over Thor's tone of voice. Was he teasing? Loki pointed at Thor and laughed. "I am not going to answer your query, Thor. I see what you're doing."

"Oh?"

"Yes...I see. If I say that I do find your wife attractive, then you are certain to assume that I will coerce her into my bed again. If I say I find her unattractive you will defend her honor and beat me to an inch of my life."

"Since when did beer make you paranoid? I am just making conversation, Loki. I am well aware that my wife has had, and probably will have, other gods and mortal men as lovers. I was surprised when she took you to her thighs, especially after all that passed between you, namely, your scissors and her hair."

"Ah, but now her hair is of spun gold that outshines the stars."

"It's in the past. I no longer dwell on such things. I feel too old and stiff to beat you much today, anyway. Just for good measure, I can provide you with a solid backhand if that would suit your masochistic needs."

Loki relaxed. "Thank you, no."

"Well, then, since they are now so firmly on my mind, I'm off to check on the thighs of Sif and see what treasures lay between them. Summon me when it is time to visit your mortal."

Loki raised his coffee mug. "Hail Thor."

"And hail Loki," Thor replied. Then under his breath added, "You bastard."

* * * *

Jada listened for the sound of her children scampering outdoors with their father as she strolled across her house in the hills to her meditation chair. It sat before an east-facing window, overlooking the Smoky Mountains. The old dark blue velveteen chair had been with her longer than her husband. At times, it was more comforting, too. She'd journeyed in it. Who knew an old overstuffed chair was a sign of wonder of the gods? Jada hung her head as she fell back into the chair. "Loki," she sighed. The god of change. The Trickster. Silvertongue. The button pusher. She glanced at the braided red cord bracelet she wore in his honor. He wanted to replace it with a ring. She caught herself shaking her head. "I can't marry you. I love you, but I cannot bind myself to you. I'm not ready to embrace that much change in my life." She closed her eyes and hummed a tonal vibration that usually helped her quickly achieve a deep meditative state. She'd avoided going deep for a while. How does one postpone vows with a god? She mustered courage. This was a deliberate summoning—unlike when he came to her in dreams. A direct summoning in meditation meant work, conversation—challenges. Dreams were almost always about sex: incredible, mind-blowing, imagination-stretching god sex. With Loki, however, there were no rules, so she could never be certain as to what she was going to meet with in the astral.

It had rained.

Just outside the window overlooking the mountains was her rainwater collection barrel. A steady drip, the perfect drum of nature, eased her into a deep meditative state. She concentrated on her breathing and let it become one with the sound of water meeting water.

He met her on the path leading into the forest flanking the entrance to the underworld. A peaceful place, she found solace in the lush, vibrant colors. She called it Elsewhere Woods. She didn't know if it had another name. Loki often met her in this place. It was not a place of work or lessons. It was a safety zone. A place for conversation. So far, he had held to that, though he often seemed disgruntled when she chose the forest over the arena or bedroom.

"Why the long face, beloved?" Loki asked.

"We need to talk." She wanted to be as matter a fact as she could, though his heady scent of honeysuckle and marijuana made her feel weak-kneed.

"Yes. We do."

Jada felt her stomach churn. His agreeing with her right off instead of doing something or saying something that would push her buttons or incite a reaction was very unlike himself.

Their bench was just up the path. Loki sometimes referred to it as their 'boning bench,' for they had made love upon it in every conceivable position. Jada didn't want to think about that right now. This was time for the bench to be for social discourse, not sexual intercourse.

If I can keep my hands off him. They sat and as always, Loki took Jada into his arms. His kisses tasted like honey, but had the effect of venom. They stung later. "What is it we need to discuss?" He kissed her chin and throat.

Jada swooned, not sure she could verbalize her thoughts and feelings in the wake of his touch. "I love you, Loki."

"I love you too." He opened her shirt. Her breasts peeked up from the confines of a slightly lacey underwire bra. "But there is something you wish to discuss with me, yes?" He freed her breasts from their fabric prison and slathered them with kisses.

"Yes. Please. But I can't with you doing that...please, Loki. Stop."

"I've missed you so, it's hard for me to not want to completely ravish you."

"We made love early this morning, Loki. We haven't been apart more than twelve hours."

"Time has little meaning to me. I go by what I feel. And I missed you." He sat back, and stroked his erect cock through his jeans. "Look what you do to me."

Jada closed her eyes and forced the chill of his touch to ebb away from her body and spirit. "I can't do this anymore, Loki. I'd like to take a break in our work. I've been afraid you might not understand."

"Oh, my sweet...I understand more than you realize. I have felt your disillusionment at the lessons I offer. I know your heart is heavy. But rest assured, I have taken steps to see that your work shall continue."

"How so?"

"Let me make love to you one final time before the next stage of your journey begins. In the haze of climax, you will come to know my plan for you." He paused. "Do you trust me, beloved?"

"I have no reason not to. For all the trials I've faced at your hands, you have never lied to me." Jada held Loki at bay for a moment. "I'm not an oathbreaker. I've just come to realize that we are not as well-suited for each other as I thought, at least for right now. I'm tired."

"I take no offense, nor do any of the gods who know of our unique arrangement. We may be emotional creatures, but we do want what is best for our people. And in this case, I think you are more suited to another trainer. Perhaps one who smells of the earth and is just as stable. I admit, I have been more of the tavern hustler to you when you needed an honorable suitor. It was not my intention to overwhelm you with my wild, quick energy. I want you to feel grounded and steady—like the beat of a drum."

"You are far more the flames of a wildfire than beat of a drum, Loki."

"Which is why we need to part, for now. After..." Jada allowed his embrace, his smooth, warm touch. She reclined against the bench, his weight atop her. Passionate kisses. Hungry kisses. She took deep breath as he concentrated on her throat. *He bit. He always bites.* She felt a trickle of blood against her flesh and his soft tongue staunch the flow and heal the wound. Where there should have been pain, she found only pleasure. She blinked and the scenery changed. He'd taken them to bed, to their forest cottage.

Clothing gone.

Arms stretched out above her.

Wrists tied to the bed frame.

Legs wide open.

Ankles tied to the footboard.

He's in one of those moods, hmmm? Jada used meditative breathing to relax her body. She knew, when Loki tied her up, that her imagination could get the best of her. It was an exercise in trust. She had to trust his godly fire. She had to trust that the bonds were only temporary.

The flames licked at her right toes first. Loki in his elemental fire was unyielding, unquelled sexual energy. The burn of desire. She'd experienced him in his true form before. He rolled along her leg. His breath singed her flesh, but did not harm her. He penetrated her with a tongue ablaze with godly energy. She cried out. From somewhere deep within the conflagration Loki's laughter roared.

He shifted and took on a more human form. He mounted her. One solid push, and he was in. Jada moaned, but found his mouth atop hers. He swallowed her pleasure as she came against his shaft.

The burn grew more intense. His hands on her breasts, on her belly. Hands of fire. An inferno of rapture. The air bolted from her lungs as waves of climax ravaged her.

Make it end! Make it end! Her frantic mind willed Loki to end his passionate libations. Immolation by Loki's love, brilliant, memorable. His sacred fire both cleansed and destroyed. True to form, he was the god of change, of new beginnings.

A cloud descended over her. Soft and cool. Loki's heat waned and the scent of freshly cut grass and subtle incense overtook her. Her body relaxed. She felt cool earth beneath her.

She caught her breath.

Her arms and legs were free, but entwined around a large body. Larger than Loki. Not smooth and lithe like Loki, but thick and strong and a bit furry. The sweet bliss of sexual union coursed through her. It wasn't Flame Hair. Long, slightly wavy red hair fell across her cheek and throat, and a red beard brushed her shoulder. Soft lips kissed. Thick cock moved within her.

She drew breath, thoughts of home, hearth and sanctuary filled her mind. This was a far different energy upon her. In her. His thrusts, this man of the earth- his thrusts quickened. She met his thrusts and felt the familiar aura of climax shoot through her in places their bodies touched. Clitoris and shaft. Bellies. Chests. Thighs.

He poured hot into her, not stifling his ecstasy.

She joined him in orgasm.

Together they reached a pinnacle of pleasure, their shared zenith far and above anything mundane or profane.

Jada exhaled and relaxed against the pillows. Her hand on her chest, she caught her breath, and giggled. "Oh, my god. Loki? That's a new trick. It was quite—unlike you."

An unfamiliar, yet gentle voice replied. "He's such a rascal, isn't he, cub? Bastard left me in a compromising position. At least it ended well for both of us."

Jada snapped to attention at the sound of the smooth voice. "You're not Loki."

"This is true. You know me, don't you, cub?"

Jada stilled her racing heart. "Why are you here? I did not offer myself to you. I have not contracted with you."

"I heard your beloved say that what you need would come in the haze of climax. Perhaps this is a bit unorthodox—even for gods—but he was true to his word. I hope you are not too alarmed by his trickery. Loki and I had a lengthy discussion about your care and feeding and your work. You are not suited to his flame, high ceremony, and veiled lessons. They lack a solid foundation. But you are suited for what I have to offer you. With me you shall dance upon solid ground, not the clouds. I am tribal, shamanic, of the earth."

"Thor. You are Thor. In lore you are not prone to taking liberties with women. Why do you invade me body and spirit now? You're no great seducer or rapist."

"Ah, I merely finished what Loki began. He took his leave at a most inopportune time. He was supposed to stay in form and allow me a taste of energy, not flee and leave me atop you. What passed between he and I and you and I is just a part of the magic of being, well—divine. Trust me, my dear. This was not supposed to be a divide-and-conquer situation, but one of embrace and comfort."

Jada slid away from the burly red-headed god. "Is this where I say hail Thor?"

"It's always good manners to praise a god."

"Hail Thor."

"I'm sure that was heartfelt in some way," he paused. "Jada, let me work with you."

"I have always trusted the gods," Jada replied. "And I know that my work may come from many sources. But I am Loki's."

"You will always be his. For now, however, will you be mine. I am as stable as the earth, yet can quake just as fiercely. I am the flash of lightning and the roll of thunder. I am the cleansing rain and rich, red soil. I am what you need. I am his gift to you."

"I know him. He will say I abandoned him. Does he feel I have abandoned him?"

Thor placed his hand over Jada's and squeezed. "It was his idea. He wants only what's best for you. In this case, me." He leaned forward and kissed her.

Jada relaxed into his embrace. His kiss fulfilled and calmed her. She felt surrounded and cushioned by cool soil. He held her, without attempting intercourse. His steady breaths reminded her of a slow beat of a drum across an open expanse. Hand to stretched skin. Sound vibration riding the current. Ancient, tribal, totemic energy passed between them. She felt the pull of deeper trance and allowed herself to be swept away into his energy.

* * * *

She was in her chair. Seated, safe, and still breathing to the rhythm of the rain.

Her mind was free. Within the trance she found Thor. He stood in the distance, a halo of blue flame, like a natural gas fire, encircling his head. He wore his battle armor and carried his symbol—the *Mjolnir*—his hammer, more than a weapon, more than an icon to a millennia of his worshippers. It was even far more than the source of his power. He was a god, a holy power, and his connectivity to the earth radiated with the strength of steel. Born of the earth, son of Jord and Odin, offspring of the goddess inhabiting the world of humankind and the All-Father, Thor was earth magic. Unstoppable, eternal. Undeniable.

Jada approached him. The will-o'-the-wisps dancing around his head ceased their intricate flame-like movements and spread out in spokes, crowning Thor. She bowed. "I am honored by your presence."

Thor chuckled. "I'm no king, cub. Don't bow to me. We shall work as equals in this realm." He held out his hand. "Will you walk with me?"

Jada took his large, calloused hand. Hers was lost inside his. "Where do we walk?" She paused. "I'm sorry. I should trust you completely and not question things."

"The lack of trust and questions come from working with Loki. He is the harbinger of butterflies in one's belly and heightened anticipatory acuity."

"And like a moth to a flame, I just kept on coming back for more. I can't say that working with him was a mistake, because I've made some doozies and I know 'em when I see 'em, but Loki is, difficult."

"Challenges always are. He is the god of change. I am the god of grounding, settling in, allowing roots to take hold."

"I hear admiration in your voice, Thor," Jada said.

"Loki is my friend. We have shared many grand adventures. I honor him. And as for our destination, I thought perhaps you might enjoy spending time with my family. After that, we'll see."

"Sif?"

"Yes, of course. And my sons and daughters—if they are at home. Did Loki take you to meet his family? In Jotunheim or Asgard?"

"I met Angrboda and Hel. He said he would take me to the cave someday, and teased me that the lessons of his cave were not easy ones."

"It's a dismal place and not one that you should fret over if you never see it. It is sorrow-ridden, and the aura of suffering is so pervasive within said cave that I believe it should be salted and sealed."

"Why has Odin not done this if the place is so haunted?"

"Loki will not allow it. He clings to that pain he suffered so grievously and, from time to time, he shares it with others, for in his eyes, catharsis can give birth to change."

"It can."

"I don't force uncomfortable changes. I help my people sink their souls into the earth and find the benefits of returning to a state of grounded bliss."

"And for this, and you, I dare say I shall be eternally grateful. Hail Loki for his wisdom in sending me Thor, god of thunder."

Thor chuckled and squeezed Jada's hand. "We'll work well together, cub."

Their walk across the vault of heaven led them to *Thrudvangr*, the field upon which Thor's hall stood. "It's *Bilskirnir*. This is your home."

"And beyond my home is all of Asgard. Come, let's hurry. I smell roasting meat. Housekeeping was alerted to your arrival. I'm sure there will be a fine repast laid out for us. And more than food—beer."

"Housekeeping?" Jada asked.

"Of course. We have paid staff in Asgard just as mortals do on Midgard. Why, Loki is husband to the overseer, the lucky bastard. My hall has 540 rooms. You don't think we have time to keep up with dusting, do you?"

"Loki and I have never discussed the minutiae of day to day life in Asgard. It seemed he always had pressing matters to which I needed to give my undivided attention."

"Like his cock?" Thor asked.

Jada snorted. "Oh, dear. Yes. But sex with Loki isn't just sex. Although I can't give you details at the moment, I'm sure the lessons I learned at the end of his penis were necessary."

"Of course they were."

Jada wasn't sure if Thor agreed with her or was being sarcastic.

"Ah, my home. Welcome to *Bilskirnir*."

Jada had to pause and soak in the breathtaking visage of *Bilskirnir*. She blinked to adjust her vision as her eyes had only just adjusted to the diffuse glow of the realm of the gods and were now blindsided by highly localized light directly before her. She realized that what appeared a modest home was but an illusion. A great glass arch reflected as if stadium lights shone upon it, but only when looking at from a slightly off-center point of view. From another point of view, the arch seemed fantastic, yes, but solid. Dead ahead, the home gave not the appearance of greatness as befitting a god, but of tasteful simplicity. A head tilt to the left or right and the absolute enormity of the place became apparent. "It's like *trompe l'oeil*. The eye is fooled. I love it. It's magic," she whispered.

"For lack of a better word, yes." He escorted her through an intricate archway made of glass. "This arch is the product of lightning against sand. Fulgurite. Petrified lightning."

"I have never seen anything like this."

"I struck my hammer against the black sand of *Vík í Mýrdal*, Iceland, in a fit of rage, mind you, and this incredibly beautiful object resulted. I knew then, that even in anger, beauty can be found."

"Anger serves its purpose. It can cleanse and renew. It doesn't always devour and suffocate."

"You have certainly been the bed wench of rage a time or two. It's good that you have not lost yourself to anger."

"I'm not going to let the bastards get me down. And they have tried. I wage a daily struggle between the motherly desire to breastfeed the world or vengeful female desire to kill it with fire. Most of the time I see the struggles for what they are, and abate my more vengeful thoughts with some kind of positive action. Sometimes, I just pour a bottle of good vodka on Loki's fire and watch the flames. I imagine they are purifying my life by burning away the layers of shit I am encased within."

"Sometimes you feel like the rug is about to be pulled out from under your feet," Thor added.

Jada nodded. "Hell, yes."

"With me, cub, you will find solid footing. Ah, Sif approaches."

Jada flustered. "I am in the home of a god and I have no offering or gift."

"Sif doesn't stand on formalities. We'll make sure you are prepared when we meet Odin. I'll have a fruit basket or something sent to him."

Jada opened her mouth to utter, "Odin likes fruit baskets?" But cut her sentence short as Thor met Sif with open arms. He then turned and pulled Jada into his embrace.

She gasped for air as he squeezed her. She felt a warm tingle against her skin where her flesh touched Sif's. It made her body giggle. Her entire frame, from crown to toes shuddered. She had to laugh. "Thor, please..."

"What's the matter cub? Can't handle a bear hug?"

Sif slapped Thor's chest. "Come on, Papa...give us our leave of your embrace so that we can introduce ourselves."

Thor gave the women one last, tremendous hug then released them. "Oh, I do love my women. So, Sif? What's for supper?"

Sif laughed. "Hail Thor. And hail Thor's appetites—for food and sex." She turned to Jada. "Come along, dear. Let's go to the kitchen and see how the meal is coming along. Give us a chance to get to know each other." Sif entwined her arm with Jada's and led her away.

Jada glanced back at Thor, who had broken into song as he relieved himself into a potted plant near the entrance.

"Thor is pissing into a plant," Jada said.

Sif shrugged. "For all his uncouth acts, Thor is, and always shall be, adorable. He's a big daddy bear."

Jada held out her right hand to Sif. "I'm Jada." She startled when the goddess hugged her instead of shaking her hand. A moment later Sif's mouth met hers. It wasn't just a peck. It was a kiss- full on and sensual. Jada tensed and clenched and her belly churned from the desire to take flight. Run away. Far away. She was in the embrace of the goddess, touched by a sacred queen.

Sif spoke against Jada's lips. "Welcome to my house."

Jada turned her head, embarrassed. "I was with Loki, but now..."

Sif chuckled. "We've all been with Loki, dear."

"I'm going to work with Thor."

"Yes, you are." Sif patted Jada's arm. "He is the eye of the storm and the storm, too. And he's said that I am the glitter caught up in the wind." Sif pulled Jada onto a padded bench off the kitchen. "Please, sit." She paused. "Thor is that, indeed. He is *la tormenta, stormurinn*. He is also the hearth fire and shelter from the storm. He is a powerful god. With Loki, the love is flammable, like brandy in a crystal goblet touched by a lit match which becomes too hot and shatters the vessel, spattering hot liquid in every direction. With Thor, love is like a heavy oaken keg which adds rich flavor to the wine and only when tapped, will it come forth and release its heady aroma. But until that moment, the wine is safely developing its deliciousness. And I am the shiny stones uncovered by the hands of one brave enough to dig into the soil of their life. I am gold, silver and mica. I am diamond, garnet and quartz. I help Thor find the hidden jewels in his wives, which he then sets to the polisher allowing them to shine in their own right."

"I am not his wife."

Sif smiled. "Let's have something to drink, shall we?"

Jada nodded. "Something stiff? Like whiskey?"

Sif nodded. "If that's what you want, yes. As you can imagine, we have a large variety of spirits in Thor's hall."

"I need a drink. I mean...I really need a drink." Sif nodded to a uniformed kitchen staff. "Whiskey."

The servant rushed over with a tray laden with a variety of blends. "I don't know which brand you prefer. Please, choose and Gretchen will pour."

Jada smiled at the servant. "Hi, Gretchen. How are you?"

The servant smiled. "I am honored to serve you your first drink in the hall of your husband."

Jada frowned. "Thor and I are not married. Have I missed something?"

Sif silenced Jada. "Just pick a whiskey, dear. We have dinner to attend to and after that, the real work starts."

Jada sighed. Her lips again tingling, she tapped the bottle of Jameson's. "I like this."

Gretchen smiled. "Right away, then."

"Sif?" Jada began. "Is something untoward at hand?"

"Only Thor if we let him drink too much with supper."

Jada took the tumbler from Gretchen and took a hard swig. She downed a second. "I see no reason to not to imbibe since I am in Asgard, astrally speaking, being led around Thor's kitchen by his wife, anticipating some serious on the job training."

"Drink away, dear. If nothing else, it will loosen you up. You are a bit tense."

"Loosen me up for what?"

"For a woman who has worked with Loki, you certainly seem innocent in the ways of the gods."

"Loki often left me in a state of flail. Shell shock. I had trouble grounding after being with him. I found it hard to relax around Loki, overall. He pushes my buttons."

"Which is why he has asked Thor to work with you. You need roots before wings. And dear, you need to relax."

I've heard that before. I've waited ten years to grow roots. What I have is a good husband, three children probably sired by Loki and the beginnings of an ulcer. "I rarely relax. Even my meditations are fraught with anxiety. Astral traveling often finds me exhausted upon my return."

"There will come a time when you accept it. Living without fear is a gift of the gods. With Thor, because he is of the earth, the paradox of corporeal, ethereal, and the spaces in-between are more blurred than with a god of fire or air. He is solid in any realm, whereas old Flame Hair might feel less so."

"I love him, you know."

"Loki? Yes. Of course you do."

"I am frightened that this is another of his cryptic lessons. A *lady or the tiger* situation. Choose a door. Be saved or be eaten. And don't freak out when you find out both doors lead to the same conclusion, tiger's jaws or not."

"I assure you, whichever door you choose in our home does not have a tiger beyond it." Sif sauntered away. "The vipers we use now are much easier to wrangle."

Vipers? Snakes? Jada held a finger aloft to question Sif, but changed her mind, swallowed her fear and continued along at the heels of the goddess.

She listened intently as Sif spoke of life at *Bilskirnir*. Though its name meant "lightning crack," the home was smoothly run and quiet. The kitchen staff paid them no heed and went on preparing huge amounts of food atop every surface. The house was quiet save for the busy hands of the cooks and echo of Thor's voice through the halls as he enjoyed his before dinner beverages. Jada found a bunch of purple carrots in a colander in a great ceramic sink and washed them.

She took a knife from the block and began slicing. "I like to cook," she said. "Cooking is a meditation for me. I swear the act of kneading bread makes my *godphone* clearer." She lifted another carrot, "Loki always speaks to me when I do repetitive tasks like dicing, chopping, slicing, and mixing."

"Ah, tasks akin to the level of work he does with his people. Loki is the god of change. He takes a simple, pure carrot and through an act of transformation, makes it a delicious meal. The dicing, chopping, slicing...that's just how mortals perceive things."

Jada raised the knife half-heartedly in salute. "Hail Loki."

"Hail Loki, indeed. I understand your love for him. I understand your exhaustion and exasperation. I know Loki quite well. Now, toss the carrots into the pot, Jada. Thor likes them."

"Just like me, huh? I fear I am being tossed into Thor's stew after being chopped up by Loki. All the king's horses and all the king's men—can they put Jada together again?"

"Nursery rhymes have little bearing on lessons learned from the gods."

Jada took a deep breath. "I smell the bread rising across the room. I know the end result will be delicious. But before it is eaten, it is mixed, imbued with fungus, punched down, kneaded, rolled, flattened, shaped and baked until there's a hard crust and soft insides." She paused. "Just like us puny mortals and the gods who love them."

"Today's bread comes from wheat threshed by Freyr's own hand. He brings Thor a bushel every Thursday morning. Thor, in return, offers Freyr honey from our hives and on Vanic holidays arranges blessings of the earth in Freyr's honor."

"Blessings?"

"Spilled seed and blood. It sweetens the soil, which in turn, reflects upon the soil of Midgard."

"I didn't know." Jada scooped the cut carrots into a bowl. "What happens on Wednesdays around here?"

Sif laughed. "Odin's day? Anything goes. He listens to petitions and makes decrees on Wednesdays. One should always bring a flagon of mead or a bottle of good aquavit when seeing Odin on a Wednesday."

"Not a fruit basket?" Jada passed off the bowl of chopped carrots to the cook.

"Odin? Fruit? Doubtful." Sig giggled. "Fruit. Goodness. Now that you've worked off some of that nervous energy you've been carrying about, shall we retire to my sitting room until supper?"

Jada nodded. "Whatever you think is best, Sif. I am a stranger here. It's better I follow your lead."

The goddess smiled. "Excellent. Come along. I think the boys are home. Would you like to meet them?"

"Magni and Modhi? Those boys?" Jada asked.

"Of course. Thor's two oldest sons. Magni's mother's, Jarnsaxa, is also one of Heimdall's mothers."

Jada laughed. "In lore Magni is stronger than Thor and is the only one able to lift the *Mjolnir*. And Modhi is the patron saint of berserkers."

"Wild and crazy, entheogen-induced battle fury. Yes. That's what my Modhi brings to the table," Sif replied.

"Do you have a designated room numbers? With 540 rooms and all...how do you keep track?"

"Well, that's the thing about divine dwellings. I can turn into any room and it will be the room I wish it to be—as long as we've crossed the threshold of the main hall and kitchen. Those two rooms never change. You know, Thor had the house bespelled after my little tryst with Loki. He wanted to make it harder for Loki to find me. Of course, the next time Loki caught up with me in the night, he cut off my hair in retaliation." Sif paused. "Oh, dear. I might as well tell you the truth. Loki did cut off my hair. It was a moment of foolishness brought on by alcohol-fueled passion. We were in bed and during climax I cut myself to feed him my blood. We got a bit carried away with the knife after that. *Blóð heift*—blood fury. It's a bit addictive. End result, I have hair of spun gold, Thor has his hammer in compensation and Loki and I keep a polite distance."

"Loki's lips were sewn shut by the dwarf who made the hammer. I have touched my tongue against each little scar. It was, at the time, almost a sacrament to do so."

"His little scars are like magnets and many beings react like steel to them."

Jada nodded. "That's Loki, all right."

"You will find Thor far more compassionate and far less threatening. Ah, we have now crossed beyond the threshold of the grand hall."

"I see no difference in the nature of this corridor."

Sif pulled Jada behind her as she pushed open a door with her foot. "The difference is subtle. Air pressure. After a time, you'll recognize it. Please, make yourself comfortable. I'll check on the boys. I smell their bubble gum in the other room, so to speak."

Jada cast eyes about the sun-filled golden-hued room. The light was only slightly diffuse by pale shades and within its glow were shades of green and coral. She chuckled at a massage chair resting before a window veiled with sheer off-white curtains. "Oh, I could use this." She sat in the chair and rested her chest and shoulders against the body rest.

"Magni here is a fine masseuse. Would you like a massage?"

Jada glanced sideways at Sif. She felt all breath leave her body as the sight of two handsome men proverbially and literally turned her head and body, around on the chair.

The men flanking Sif were obvious products of Thor, with reddish hair and beards, broad shoulders, regal bearing, sly smiles, and bedroom eyes. Both had the cool, collected aura of their stepmother.

"I am Magni, and I am happy to work out any kinks you may have. Please, make yourself comfortable in the chair."

Jada felt her cheeks flush. "I don't really—"

"Yes. Yes, you do." Magni looked insistent.

She turned around on the bench and assumed the position.

"Can you remove your shirt, dearest Jada?" Sif giggled.

"I don't think I can."

"It has glued itself to you? Let me help you remove it," Magni offered.

Jada held her breath as his large hands stripped her of light sweater and t-shirt. He unhooked her bra.

"Oh, dear god," Jada said. "I..."

Strong, warm hands grasped her shoulders. "I fit the description of a dear god. What can I do for you?"

"I'm working with Thor," she said. "And I love Loki."

"Of course you are here to work with father. Do you think that receiving a massage will in any way change that?" He then whispered. "And we all love Loki—or have after too much wine."

She quivered as his fingertips worked their way down her spine. An involuntary moan escaped her lips. "I'm sorry," she whispered.

"No need for shame or remorse in Thor's house. If you find pleasure as well as healing in my touch, then my job is well-done."

Magni's brother laughed. "And by the rise in his slacks I'd say he'll need to finish the job later."

Jada couldn't see the smack of Sif's hand against Modhi's shoulder, but heard it and the reprimand clear enough. "Modhi, your brother is his father's son and his arousal is only natural."

"Yes, mother. But what about mine? I have no skill as a masseuse and thereby am unlikely to coax one of father's women from her shirt this fine day. I dare say she is a comely mortal. Father must be very happy when between her thighs."

"I can hear you," Jada called, her head still turned away as she slipped into a heavenly state of relaxation.

"Pay Modhi no heed, Jada. Thankfully, your work with Thor does not involve his sons or daughters. Our daughter, Thrud is, at least, polite to guests. She is not at home today, however. She has a suitor and they are away in *Alfheim*. Go wash up for supper, Modhi," Sif commanded.

"Mother, I am not a child," he replied.

Sif struck his shoulder again. "Then quit acting like one."

Jada gasped as Magni put pressure next to her right shoulder blade. "Jesus Christ."

"He isn't here, dear. I believe father invited him to Yule once, but he wasn't able to make it."

"What?"

Magni leaned closer, applying more weight against her back. "Godly humor. Feel better, Jada?"

"Oh, yes. I didn't realize how tense I was."

"You're still tense, though I think your physical self must be asleep now, well-fucked and well-sated. But I don't smell father on you. I think another was with you, lucky bastard. I sometimes envy the work mortals do with the divine." Magni rubbed his large hands outward from the center of Jada's back, as if brushing away sand. "Done. Please don't dress on my account." "Magni—" Sif said.

"I'll see you at supper Magni. Thank you for the massage." Her back still turned, she donned her bra and shirt.

The lights flickered.

Modhi laughed. "Ah, saved by the bell, or silent call to the table in this case. It's supper time."

* * * *

The table setting was far from opulent. Though she was in the house of a god, and expected a bit of *bling*, Jada was pleasantly surprised to find stoneware plates and ordinary flatware. The dining hall had a rustic, homespun feel to it. A great hearth, alive with flame roared in the background as Thor's family came to supper. Sif motioned for Jada to take a seat to the left of the head of the table. She, herself, sat on the right. Magni and Modhi didn't wait for their father to sit, but boisterously filled their plates from the platters set out on the table.

Jada felt a sudden shift in the mood of the room as heavy footfalls neared. There was an overpowering electrical current preceding the diner. She knew that prickle. Loki. "Sif," she began, panic punching her, "Loki. Thor invited Loki?"

Sif shrugged. "It will be fine, dear. Loki is always on his best behavior when in our house. I've shown him my needle and thread and he knows I'm not afraid to sew his mouth shut if he becomes offensive."

Jada shuddered. "I fear a retelling of the *Lokesenna*. I don't want my dirty laundry aired."

Sif's calm voice soothed her a bit. "If you have any skeletons in your closet, Thor is already aware of them, to be sure."

He doesn't know everything. Even Loki doesn't know everything. "I'm not sure I can do this."

"Do what?" The voice carried across the room as sweet as honey and twice as smooth.

Jada's recently relaxed shoulder blades locked up as Loki took the chair beside her. She didn't look at him. His ability to read her mind alarmed her.

Thor greeted Sif first. She rose to meet him and they embraced.

"Hail Thor," she said. Jada watched as Thor stroked Sif's long golden braid. His hands were on his wife, but his eyes...were on her.

He came to her next, quietly nodding to his sons. Thor offered Jada his large hand and pulled her to her feet. He kissed her. She let him.

Loki cleared his throat and Thor released her. The thunder god spoke with stern tone. "I am this woman's patron. I work with her in this house. Do you hear me boys?"

Magni and Modhi answered in unison, "Yes, sir." "And you, son of Laufey, I claim Jada. She is now mine." Loki smirked.

Jada wanted to sink into a hole and die.

"She will always be mine, Thor. My mark is upon her and in her. But I recognize your claim and respect the work you shall do with her. Just know that your lessons might become blurred with those from my repertoire. I do leave a bit of an impression. A lasting memory."

"I will not have this meal become a *flyting*, Loki. I must ask that you fill your mouth with cook's good food instead of exhaling sly comments."

Loki chuckled. "Yes, Sif. I bow to the wishes of the mistress of the house."

Jada sat. Sat on a hot seat as Loki's electric energy reached out for her like carnivorous tendrils. His gaze unnerved her. "Please don't stare at me, Loki."

He passed her a platter of warm bread. "I see Thor's touch at work in you. Do you enjoy hammer time with him? Or do you miss my pillar of flame?"

Jada lashed out. "We haven't been intimate, Loki. Except for your little trick wherein you left Thor with me—and you left without so much as a goodbye."

"Leave Jada alone, Loki. You are a guest in my house and I will not have you taunting her. Leave your feelings of jealousy and abandonment to your own table."

"It's not that I feel jealous or abandoned. Well, I guess I do in some sense-even though I know our separation is temporary. I just hate letting go of beautiful things."

"I'm not a thing," Jada said. And I haven't abandoned you. I love you, you son of a bitch. I just can't keep walking across the coals. I need a break.

She could see the torch Loki carried for her in his eyes. He had heard her thoughts.

"Of course you're not. It's a figure of speech, dear one. Rarely have I experienced separation anxiety such as this."

Jada dramatically stabbed a potato and ripped it open with her fork and knife. "We have discussed this before, Loki. It's not always about you."

Thor laughed. "She's got you there, Trickster. You have a way of making everything about you, but she's right. Oh, cub, you are a clever woman."

Loki reached across the table for the wine. He poured his glass to the brim. He took a drink and swallowed hard. "So, when's the wedding?"

Jada startled. "Wedding?"

Loki cackled over his wine.

Thor cleared his throat. "I'm sorry, Jada. Some of our work is so intense that it can only happen between husband and wife. Ours will be a short-term contract, of course. I understand and accept that Loki has your heart." Thor looked up over his own glass and shot Loki an intense glare. "Being a godspouse is both a part of the work and the work, itself."

"When I married my mortal spouse, I vowed in my heart to become Loki's bride." Loki shook his head. "We did not take formal vows. And even had we done so, it would not prevent you from marrying Thor. Our relationship shall someday build upon the foundation he creates with you. Accept his proposal and become a *Thorswoman*. I will not stand in the way."

Jada bit her lip and tried to shake off the heavy flush coursing through her chest, neck and face. "I..."

Sif struck Thor in the shoulder. "You are as about as romantic as a mackerel."

Thor's shoulders fell. "Oh, dear. I've displeased Sif. The wives do sometimes conspire together to bring out the best in us, don't they Laufeyjarsson?"

Loki nodded and made a mock toast toward Sif, then Jada. "Indeed."

Thor rose. Facing Jada he said softly, "My lady, do me the honor of becoming my wife. It is in name only—a marriage of convenience per se. But I promise, nevertheless, to honor you and help your roots grow deep before he pulls you to the stars."

Sif snarled. "That is a command, not a proposal."

"Yes, Thor," Loki began. "Say it sweetly. Forget that lug of a brain you carry around and use your heart. Think of how she will remember this day years from now."

"So unlike you to look to someone else's needs. Is this a new Loki at my table?" Sif asked. Then under her breath added, "Hold back, boys. Uncle Loki is just teasing daddy. No insult intended."

Loki snickered. "Dearest Sif, I am wiser in my old age and thereby have learned that every now and then the best way to get my way is to allow others to have theirs. And no offense intended, boys. Back down, you look like Rottweilers."

The thunder god cleared his throat. "Will you have me? Will you be my wife?"

Jada closed herself to the table's activity. All eyes were on her. She knew it. She focused on a single piece of purple carrot peeking through the crust of the stew. Its edges were brown from heat, but its vibrant color still offered an invitation to taste.

It was singed around the edges, but still full of flavor. *I am the carrot. Thor is the gravy that binds the stew into the pastry. Sif is the salt. Loki is the fire. Together, we are a meal, the parts that make the whole. Alone, I'm just a carrot, dangling precariously before progress. I can't offer more to this relationship than what I am, and what I am is splintered. It's time I grew a pair and faced that which keeps me small and intimidated. My foundation shall falter if I don't allow myself to put down roots. I won't have the strength to push through the soil to face the sun. It's time to step out of the shadows.*

Jada exhaled sharply and drew in a deep breath, filling her lungs. "Thor, you are the warmth of a hearth fire and the very shelter that gives it sanctuary. You approach me respectfully and treat me honorably. I feel safe with you. I will work with you. And I will be your wife for the duration of that work. But know this, my heart belongs to Loki. My heart will always belong to Loki. Though he may cause me to pluck it out and burn it black for his supper, I will love him."

Thor raised his glass. "We all love Loki, dear. Our threats to sew his lips shut and lop off his head are mere foreplay." He took a brief sip, then held it out again. "And thereby, it is done. We do not stand on formalities here. We are now husband and wife by oral contract, before these witnesses. I look forward to our wedding night, for what is a marriage without a marriage bed? But, my dear...I fear that will have to wait, for I hear words left unsaid."

Jada nodded. "I want this to be right. I feel from you that I can advance spiritually under your tutelage. I think, first, however, that I need to accomplish something. A task—an ordeal, if you will."

"What would that be?" Thor's voice was strained. "It is my father who is master of cathartic ordeals, not I."

Jada turned in her chair to face Loki. "I want to face my demons." "Why look to me for such a feat?" Loki asked.

"You are the harbinger of change. I may prefer Thor's gentle ways, but it is true that only you who can guide me into darkness, though the way out of that pit is my own to find."

"My cave. You want enter my cave to embrace suffering."

Jada nodded. "To embrace it, and conquer it. Only after purging the horrors of my past can I work properly with Thor and walk the path he shall set out for me." She turned to Thor. "You are all that is good, Thor. I cannot embrace our relationship while a thick wall of fear and resentment divide me from you."

Thor sighed. "I fear for your safety. That place is—unholy. But your statement proves that my desire for your well-being is already at hand."

Sif rose. "Hail Jada, sisterwife, embracer of darkness, the woman who creates her own lighted path." She grasped a handful of her own silken yellow hair and pulled hard. She winced, but didn't hesitate. She removed several long strands and rolled them between her palms. "With this ring, fashioned of my flesh and blood, imbued with the magic of pure gold spun on the looms of dark elves, I honor you. A gift. May it fill your veins with courage and wisdom as you walk the path of horrors past." She held out her hand and offered a gold band to Jada. "I hope, Jada, that when you return from the lair of the serpent, that you will honor us all by giving voice to your true name."

Jada removed the ring from Sif's palm. "I don't know what you mean."

Thor chuckled. "You hide your name—even from yourself. How long has it been since you said it aloud? What evil tied your tongue to your true identity?"

Jada slipped on the ring and reached up to wipe away a single tear. "It was evil. It was. It's name was father."

Thor covered his face with his hands. "Oh, cub, I am sorry."

Loki snarled. "I knew it. You never voiced it, but I knew it. That is what blocked our work, and our love."

Jada nodded. "I'd like to go now, while I feel powerful, and before I allow another moment to pass in the shadow of his abuse."

Loki pushed away from the table. "Tell your new husband goodbye and let's away."

Jada looked to Sif, who bowed her head reverently. "I wish you success, sisterwife."

Thor took one great step and scooped Jada into his arms. "I can offer you one thing to help ease your travels."

Jada pressed her head against his chest. "What's that?"

"Divinity." Thor stepped back and picked up a steak knife. He sliced open his hand and offered the pooling blood to Jada. "Drink. Be one with the *Aesir*. When my blood flows in your veins your life force is infused with a roll of thunder and crack of lightning."

Jada suppressed a squeamish gag reflex as she put her lips to the pool of blood in Thor's palm. The smooth, warm coppery dark red nectar coated her tongue and slid down her throat. She shivered as the power of a god cascaded through her core. A surge shook her much like an orgasm. She lifted her face and looked into his. "Hail Thor."

He kissed her ruby lips. "Be safe. Embrace, conquer, and return to me."

Jada relished the heat which pulsed between them. "I just took root."

"You took footing to bedrock when you accepted me as your patron. Hail Jada, she whose provenance I shall watch over, protect and purify."

Jada whispered, "Thank you, Thor." She glanced over her shoulder at Loki. "I'm ready. Let's do this."

* * * *

Loki guided Jada from the Thor's house.

"We're being shadowed," Jada said. She pulled her arm away each time Loki tried to take it.

"I know. It's their way. They will accompany me until I am off Thor's land." Loki raised his voice. "IT'S NOT LIKE THEY DON'T TRUST ME." Magni and Modhi chuckled behind them.

"How far is it?" Jada asked.

"We'll need transportation. It isn't close."

"What? Gonna call a cab?"

Loki put two fingers to his lips and whistled. "My son."

Jada stopped. "Son? I'm going to ride a wolf? A serpent?"

Loki shook his head. "Sleipnir, dear."

"The eight-legged horse you birthed when in equine form—yes. I know the story. I know of Sleipnir. You saved the sun, moon, and Freyja by shapeshifting and gendershifting into a mare. Pretty impressive." She mock saluted Him. "But I thought he was Odin's, no?"

"I gave him to Odin, but as his mother, so to speak, I get perks."

"I like horses."

"Then you'll love Sleipnir. Be aware, however, that his gait feels a bit un-

even at first. You will grow accustomed to it."

"Mother!" A lanky man with platinum blond hair jogged up to them.

Jada whispered. "I could ride that."

Loki elbowed her. "We've shared a woman before. If you want to take the time—"

"Tempting." She sized up the handsome man before her. "You're Sleipnir?"

Loki leaned in. "He's full Jotun, dear, and thereby a shapeshifter."

"Yes, dear lady. I am Sleipnir. Can I give you a lift?"

"We're going to my cave, son."

"Oh, mother. That is a dismal place to take such a lovely woman. Let's go to *Alfheim* instead. The realm of the bright elves is always pleasant this time of year."

Loki placed a hand on his son's shoulder. "Not this time. We need swift and sure passage to the end of all the worlds. Do you remember the way?"

"I carried you home after your long confinement. I remember." Sleipnir shook his head. His long white hair whirled about, creating a veil of energy which covered him from head to toe. From the sparkling white whirlwind emerged a horse so brilliant its coat rivaled that of the sun.

The great beast knelt, its front legs and head bowing.

Loki stroked the horse's mane. "You honor us, my son." He mounted easily. "Come along, Jada. Don't leave an eight-legged horse down on his front four for too long. It looks fabulous, but can get a bit uncomfortable."

"Bareback, huh?" Jada took Loki's hand and mounted. As Sleipnir rose, she wrapped her arms around his waist. She buried her face in his back and held on for dear life.

The experience reminded her of riding a bullet train: scary fast. She'd gone on horseback before, mostly English Pleasure style, and once or twice western trail riding. This was a combination of both styles, plus. The plus was definitely unique to an eight-legged horse that could tread both earth and sky.

"Not that I mind your embrace or the sensation of your face buried between my shoulder blades, dear, but you should open your eyes and pay attention. The view is magnificent."

Jada couldn't pull her face out of Loki's jacket. She made a muffled reply. "I'm all right for now. No problems. No worries. I'm about to face my worst fears and causes of anxiety, but damn, I'm good."

Loki chuckled. "As you wish, Jada. I'll take you on horseback again someday."

She didn't reply. She'd been riding with Loki a number of times—just not on horseback. Thinking of sex with him was a memory that elicited both great desire and true terror. Loki did not make much distinction between love making and lessons. Sometimes the lessons were whispered into her ear during intercourse. It had worn her out. Still, holding him, his red hair tickling her face...was more than just a little arousing.

She reached her right hand down Loki's tight stomach and slid her fingers inside his pants at the waist.

Never shy, he deftly unzipped his fly. Freed from constraint, his engorged member sprung up to meet Jada's fingers.

She smoothed two fingers over his head in a circular motion. She pressed inward and palmed his shaft to stroke him.

Loki chuckled. "I've missed you, Jada."

"Don't get any ideas. It's the motion of the ocean, Loki. Sleipnir is one titillating ride."

Sleipnir slowed from gallop to walk. After a few long strides of his eight legs, he stopped. In a burst of firefly-like lights, Sleipnir shifted to male, his passengers safely aground.

Jada had not forgotten Loki's cock. She tightened her grip and stroked. Loki rolled his head and let it fall backward, his long braid cascading down his back to his hips. He moaned and planted his feet firmly as his erection grew.

"I see you have taken control of my mother. How does this aid your cause, Jada?" Sleipnir unfastened the top button on his bell bottom jeans.

"I need to keep a steady head where I'm going. If I can't think of anything else besides his cock inside me, I might as well pack up and go home now."

Loki chuckled. "For sanity's sake, kneel." He put his hands atop Jada's head and coaxed her to her knees.

His cock tasted familiar. She knew the shape of his head as it emerged from its sheathe from memory. Muscle memory. She had a strong tongue muscle. She had learned over their many erotic encounters how to fellate him in such a way that made his fiery eyes roll back in his head and his legs quiver.

Jada stroked her hand along his shaft and let her mouth slide farther and farther toward the base. She took him as deeply down her throat as she could, then quickened the pace of her hand. The curl of her index finger and thumb hit her lips with each pass.

As Loki's salt welled, she pulled away and laughed. "So, Sleipnir—you just going to stand there with your hands in your pockets or are you going to ante up?"

"I'm invited to this party? Lovely! Always a spectator and never on the team gets so old."

Loki moaned. "You're killing me Jada. I am engorged beyond reason. Either finish me with that sweet mouth of yours or let me have at you. I promise I shall not leave you wanting."

Jada fell back onto the grassy tundra and waved Loki and Sleipnir to her.

She closed her eyes and let them touch her as they wished.

Beyond the veil of her tightly shut eyes she beheld the white energy of orgasm and the air around her smelled of honeysuckle.

Hands rolled her and urged her to her knees. Strong hands lifted her and placed her against the hardness she knew well.

Jada opened her eyes and mounted Loki.

She laughed as Sleipnir pushed her forward and breached her rear. Wetness from her own readiness had spread and lubricated her. His passage was far from unpleasant.

She fell into the rhythm of Sleipnir's thrusts, riding Loki to the beat.

Loki cawed like a crow, reached up and slapped Sleipnir's shoulder. "That's my boy. Give it to her with that horse leg of yours."

"Your cock is no less impressive. She'll remember this shared orgasm for the rest of her life."

"She certainly won't feel the need for relations anytime soon. I bet when fantasies overshadow her meditations, they will not be about sex."

"Just shut up," Jada whispered, out of breath. She bore down against Loki as they climaxed in tandem and lunged back to capture Sleipnir as he shot hot inside her.

Entwined and sweat-soaked bodies reclined into the tall grasses. Jada placed a hand atop her chest, willing her heart to slow. "That'll wake you up in the morning."

Sleipnir chuckled. "Ridden hard and put away wet."

Loki pulled himself to his feet. "Another job well done. Anxiety alleviated, mind cleared, and body strengthened ten-fold by a good jolt of godly prowess. My work here is done."

"How much farther is it?" Jada asked, as she gathered her clothing.

"Not far. Do you see the foothills at the edge of this expanse? They glow such a lovely shade of purple at dusk. My cave is there."

Sleipnir shimmered. He nickered as he took his stallion form and motioned his head in a way that clearly said *hurry up*.

Loki mounted easily, and lifted Jada up to ride in front of him. "I am loathe to say that any time spent at your thighs is wasted, but let's proceed with the task at hand and not succumb to any further dalliances of a carnal nature, hmm?"

Jada laughed. "I had needs. I'm good now."

Loki pressed his heels into Sleipnir and the trio took off.

The distant hills seemed less distant only minutes into the journey.

Jada held on to Sleipnir's mane and tried not to compare the ride to sitting in the front of a roller coaster, but was what it felt like: heart-in-throat, stomach-in-knots, and blood running-cold. As the purple hills grew near, her resolve grew stronger. *Thor is too pure; too decent to be sullied by the shadows of my past. I will embrace the fear and pain and be victorious over them. I will. I am. By this journey I have already defeated my abusers. Hail Thor. Hail Loki. And thank you, Jimmy, my mortal spouse, for understanding the work I do with the gods.*

As she completed her thought—a brief moment of gratitude toward the men in her life, her stomach lurched. She turned to vomit, and realized she was standing, not riding, and alone, not protected by godshifter forces, and at the entrance to a cave.

Jada felt the blood rush from her extremities and for a moment she thought she would keel over. She took a deep breath and forced herself upright.

She had nothing to carry with her except painful memories, untapped rage, welling passions and faith—faith in the gods, and even more importantly, faith in herself.

* * * *

The journey of a thousand miles begins with a single step. No amount of therapy, positive affirmations, mystic quotes, or willpower could make her take the three necessary steps into the cave entrance. She took steps fueled by pure adrenaline.

Her post coital heart rate hadn't yet slowed. She thought it might burst through her chest as her toes graced the edge of the natural light at the mouth of the cave.

Her eyes slowly adjusted to the shadows and gloom of Loki's torture chamber. Three jagged rocks rose up from the floor just right of center. Even in the half-light she saw their sides were stained red. Giant claw marks flanked another stain on the wall near her. Something big had killed something small, and ripped it apart. A broken pottery bowl had been cast into the wall opposite the claw marks. The shards were thick with dust, but the yellow glaze still vibrated with the only sensation not marked by doom before her. The bowl radiated a heartbeat like a pulse, true and steady.

"Sigyn's bowl," Jada whispered. She scooped up the largest of the shards and in her left hand held it before her like a shield. She prayed, "Sigyn, may your mystic stamina in adverse situations strengthen me now." She took a step toward the bloodstained wall and placed her right palm against it. "Hail, Narvi and Vali, sons of Loki and Sigyn, unwitting and innocent pawns in the games of fate the gods played. May your innocence strengthen that which I lost as a child so that I can again grasp magic."

The blood splattered on the wall wet her hand. *The blood of the innocent never dried.* It sickened her. The gods had not been kind of Loki's family. One son had been forced to slaughter the other. The entrails of the slain were used to bind Loki to the jagged rocks jutting up like razors from the cave floor with a spitting viper above his head. And Sigyn, his wife, out of duty or love or godly request—had caught the venom of the serpent as it dripped upon Loki's face. And now the bowl sat here, cast aside and broken.

Jada moved the shard into her bloodied palm. The everlasting love of mother to child permeated her. She shivered. There is no more powerful a shield than that which a mother can provide out of love for her children. "Your thoughts disgust me."

Jada went cold. A thousand dire memories surfaced. The desire to run and hide overtook her. Duck, cover, be unseen. Untouched. "Father," she said softly.

"Why are you in this filthy place?" His voice always cut with disdain. "Still rolling in the muck, are you? I should have strangled you in your crib rather than see my good name tarnished by your unclean choices."

Jada smelled his sour breath against her neck. Father always reeked of cheap whiskey. Even in death the embalmers couldn't alleviate the odor. She took a deep breath and forcefully exhaled the foulness her father's spirit carried with him. "Don't talk to me that way, father."

The spirit of her father pin-prickled its way around her body. It hurt. It hurt like the memories of abuse he'd given her as his legacy. "Ungrateful bitch. You never did learn the lessons presented to you."

"How could any child learn lessons at the end of a broken whiskey bottle?"

"Your sister learned. Your brother, too. But not you. Not my little jewel. My baby."

"You were wrong to do those things to us."

"Wrong?"

"Yes."

The malicious spirit's jagged surface pressed into her. "You best speak respectfully to me, little girl, or I will punish you. It's been a long time, but I haven't forgotten how. Have you?"

"No."

The shadow softened. "You liked it."

"No."

"You said you did."

Jada shuddered. "You made me say it. You forced me to praise you. As you robbed me of my innocence and childhood and virginity...you—"

The shadow rippled and took on a shell similar to the quills of a hedgehog. "If I hadn't taught you, you just would have gone out and learned from some other man."

"I was a child."

The shadow made a slurping sound. "A delicious child."

"I still bear the scars of your little blood rituals."

"Use that broken piece of pottery and feed me some of your blood now. Cut yourself."

Jada didn't move.

"I said now, little jewel."

"The day I buried you I vowed I would never cut myself again to feed your insane appetite or anyone else's. What father buys his seven-year-old daughter a knife set? You knew I would hurt myself. You were waiting for that first cut. Let daddy kiss it. You sick bastard."

"I produced children to meet my needs, not for the betterment of society. Call me whatever you want. The fact still remains...you liked it. You swooned into the arms of my patron beings and wanted them as much as I wanted you."

Jada did not want to fall into her father's trap of word games. He had been a master of convolution and control. His spirit was no different. "I'm not here to discuss the lies you tell."

"So, why are you here?"

"Self-exorcism."

She lashed out and pulled her father's spirit into her arms. Its quills ripped her flesh and the smell caused bile to rise in her throat. She opened her mouth and vomited on the shadow she held. It rippled and moaned. She didn't care. He didn't deserve anything more from her than vomit. Even that was too good for him.

"Every child deserves to be loved and respected. You gave us nothing even remotely related to that. You destroyed my childhood. You destroyed my ability to love. You are the stuff of nightmares and are an unclean stain on my soul." She pushed the shadow away. Its quills stuck and pulled her skin painfully before dislodging. She winced and glanced at her bare arms, now polka-dotted with blood. "And through my torture and abuse I have come to realize that I am perhaps the most blessed woman on the face of the earth. I survived. I am loved by both a man and a god, and I will do my work and live my life unhindered by the shackles you placed upon me when I was little. Your hold on me ends now." She paused. "I was not born to feed your lust for blood and innocence. I rebuke and renounce your patron spirits for the evil schizophrenic visions they are."

"I always did love it when you fought back." The shade of her father lunged forward like cracked whip. Jada couldn't deflect the blow as it struck her hard across the face. Hands of black mold pawed at her breasts. Diseased fingers closed around her throat.

She held the shard aloft, transfixed by loss of air, the crush of pain, the disgust of his touch. As consciousness fled a softly lit visage of Sigyn rose up from the yellow fragment. Jada focused on that...on the face of the woman who stood by Loki when no-one else would. Steady, patient, honorable Sigyn, who quelled the suffering of her husband with stamina which could only spring from love and forgiveness.

Love and forgiveness.

With her final moment of life passing, Jada enveloped the dark spirit of her abusive, pseudo-vampiric father in an embrace. She mouthed three simple, powerful, cleansing words. *I forgive you.*

Though no sound ushered forth from her crushed windpipe and the thread of her life hung by a single fiber, in that moment, Jada knew she was more powerful than the trauma and rage she had carried around like a cancerous tumor. Where she once wished only to see her father flayed alive and entrails burned, she now felt pity.

Jada shed a layer of skin saturated with fear, indecision and guilt. She brought the round edge of the bowl down hard against the essence of her father.

The sound of fingernails on a chalkboard followed by the popping of bubble wrap filled the cave. It echoed through the jagged rocks to which Loki had been bound. It bounced off the stains of his children's blood. It infiltrated the spirit of her father and she felt it implode against her chest.

Arms now emptied of father, she found her embrace now encircled her own shaken form. She fell to her knees and gasped for air. Her throat burned, but swallowed the life-giving oxygen. A thousand fireflies of liquid light rained down from the vault of the cave. Instinctively, she held the piece of Sigyn's bowl up and out, to catch the remnants of her past now draining away like water down a sink. The small concave piece of pottery acted as a catchment and when full, with a turn of her wrist, she emptied it. Emptied the pain. Emptied the vessel which had shielded her true self since childhood.

And rose up anew.

Jada watched the last of the fire drops fall to the cave floor and dissipate. She coughed, thankful for the sound that emitted from her vocal chords. Raspy and weak, she uttered her true name into the darkness. "Julie." She placed her palms together and bowed toward the pillars.

She bowed toward the blood-stained wall and still holding the shard, emerged from the cave.

Loki swooped her into his arms and lifted her onto Sleipnir. "What did you leave behind?"

She cleared her throat. "Jada."

"Do you wish to keep the shard of Sigyn's bowl or can I toss it back into the cave? I find it disturbing."

"It saved you from having that pretty face of your further scarred and you would not keep it as a treasure in that little dragon's hoard of special items you have? I'm certain my best bra is there."

Loki laughed. "Yes, actually, it is."

"Keep the bra, since I'm sure you rubbed your junk against it. I'll keep the shard."

"Only when I miss you, dear. But I truly do not wish to keep any part of that bowl. Down to the smallest speck of dust that falls from it, I want it far away from me," he replied.

"I'm going to keep it, Loki. It is a powerful weapon in its own right."

"Will you have use of a weapon in the wake of your victory over the spirit of that asshat you called father?"

Julie nodded. "My journey is just beginning. I'm grateful that this shard, which represents all the best things between a wife and her husband is going with me and not a ton of soiled baggage connected to my soul by chains forged from denial and self-loathing." She paused to scoot up against Loki as Sleipnir rose. "I may need the shard to remember the good things between husband and wife."

"Hail Thor," Loki said softly.

"And hail Loki."

He chuckled. "You will have me?"

"Oh, yes. With Thor's stability and your passion, I can't go wrong. I see that now."

"I love you, Julie," Loki replied. "I've always known your true name, but until this moment, feared using it. You did your best to keep hidden. Thor and I could barely see through your veil. I use it now to honor you and your victory. Hail, Julie, woman of virtue and victory, who shall be my wife." She pressed her face into Loki's shoulder blades as Sleipnir took off.

Dawn had risen.

She smelled sweet spices and vanilla on the wind. Someone had baked a wedding cake. Her stomach growled. She was hungry for all the sweet things her new life had to offer. She chuckled, enjoying the flow of energy coursing through her. "I am inspired, Loki. I am blessed, and in those blessings, both from the gods and those claimed by my own hands, I feel I am obligated to share my gifts, both material and spiritual, with others. I feel strong enough now to learn and share the lessons of gods to mortal and husbands to wife and human to humanity."

"Let your work commence, Julie. Let that which was dulled and hidden, stand polished in the light."

"I am polished by your fire."

"You are a precious jewel born deep in the earth and bound to it by the will of that blustering thunder god. You are Thor's jewel, tempered and pressed into brilliance by flames. Flames can burn away debris and reveal facets yet unseen in even the most delicate of gems."

"I can take the heat now, Loki."

Loki chuckled, low and throaty. "I aim to see just how hot we can make things."

"I have the distinct feeling I've a wedding night with Thor pending. Come to us later, after midnight, perhaps before dawn. I want you and Thor to..."

"Put you through the rock tumbler?"

Julie smiled. "Yes. And put it on high."

ABOUT THE AUTHOR

Darragha Foster is the author of the award-winning paranormal romance novel, *The Orca King*, as well as several other novels of a similar nature. She loves scary movies, her miniature dachshund, and her iPhone (which she claims changed her life). She has been married for over twenty years to her mate from the infinite past, a very patient man who doesn't mind being her crash-test dummy for love scenes. Her favorite quote is from the writings of Nichiren Daishonin: *Many raging fires are quenched by a single shower of rain.* Darragha is all about joy, and hopes she shares a bit of the same with her readers at every turn of the paper or electronic page.